Thomas, Percy and the Funfair

Based on *The Railway Series* by The Rev. W. Awdry

First published in Great Britain 2008 by Egmont UK Limited

239 Kensington High Street, London W8 6SA

HiT entertainment

Thomas the Tank Engine & Friends™

CREATED BY BRITT ALLCROFT

Based on The Railway Series by The Reverend W Awdry
© 2008 Gullane (Thomas) LLC. A HIT Entertainment Company

Thomas the Tank Engine & Friends and Thomas & Friends are trademarks of Gullane (Thomas) Limited.
Thomas the Tank Engine & Friends and Design is Reg. US. Pat. & Tm. Off.

ISBN 978 1 4052 3868 7

1 3 5 7 9 10 8 6 4 2

Printed in China

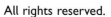

It was a beautiful morning on the Island of Sodor.

It was the day of The Fat Controller's funfair.
There would be fireworks and fairground rides
for all the children.

There was to be a special visit from the Chinese
Dragon too. Percy was delighted. He thought the
Chinese Dragon was the most exciting thing of all.

The Fat Controller arrived at Tidmouth Sheds.
He had come to give the engines their jobs.

"Edward," he said, "you will pull the merry-go-round.
Henry, you will pull the roller-coaster. Gordon will
take the fairground people and Toby, the bumper
cars. James and Emily will take the Ferris Wheel.
And Thomas," he boomed, "you are to collect the
fireworks and the Chinese Dragon."

"What's my job, Sir?" asked Percy, hopefully.

"You are to collect the coal from the Coal Plant and take it to all the stations," ordered The Fat Controller. "A railway can't run without coal. It's a very important job."

The Fat Controller left and all the engines were very excited . . . except Percy. He felt very left out.

Percy chuffed sadly over to the Coal Plant. This didn't feel like a very important job at all.

When he arrived, there was a long line of trucks. "I wish I was pulling something exciting," he grumbled. "Not boring old trucks!"

So, he left the trucks and pulled out of the Coal Plant.

Along the line, Percy met Toby. He puffed past, pulling brightly coloured bumper cars. The children in a nearby school clapped and cheered.

Then, Edward chuffed past with the merry-go-round. The children cheered even louder.

Percy thought that Toby and Edward were having a wonderful time.

Suddenly, an idea flew into Percy's funnel!

"Maybe Edward and Toby need some help? Helping friends is much more important than delivering coal!" he wheeshed.

So, Percy forgot all about the trucks at the Coal Plant. He steamed away after his friends instead.

Toby and Edward had stopped at a red signal.
Percy puffed up alongside.

"Do you need any help?" he peeped.

"No, thank you, Percy," said Toby.

"We can do it!" chuffed Edward.

Percy was sad. He wanted to do something for the
funfair too.

Further up the line, Percy saw James and Emily stopped at a Crossing. They were taking the Ferris Wheel.

"That looks like fun!" thought Percy. "I'm sure they'll need some help."

But James and Emily didn't need any help either.

Percy felt very upset. Then, he saw Gordon waiting at a signal.

Gordon was pulling the fairground people. But he didn't need any help.

"Goodbye, little Percy," he said, and wheeshed away.

Then, Percy saw Henry on the bridge above. He was pulling the roller-coaster.

"That must be really exciting," peeped Percy. "I am sure Henry would like some help."

But Henry didn't need any help either.

Percy chuffed away slowly. He was really glum now.

He found Thomas waiting at the next signal. Thomas was carrying the fireworks and the Chinese Dragon.

"That looks like the most fun of all!" gasped Percy.

But Thomas didn't need any help pulling the Chinese Dragon, and whooshed straight past Percy.

Percy had forgotten all about his important job.
And now, there was trouble . . .

James was stuck on the line. "There's no coal at the
stations!" he called to Percy. "We've all run out!"

"Oh, no!" cried Percy. "If the engines don't get some
coal, the funfair won't open. Then all the children will
be sad. And it will all be my fault!"

Percy knew what he had to do. He had to pick up his trucks and take the coal to the stations as quickly as he could.

Percy wheeshed all over the Island, delivering coal to his friends. Now, he was really able to help them.

Soon, everyone's boilers were bubbling! The engines were back to full speed.

They all thanked Percy for his help.

"Thank you, Percy!" they all whistled.

"See you at the funfair," peeped Thomas.

It was getting late when Percy finished his last delivery of coal.

He arrived at the funfair just as the fireworks began. The rockets soared high into the sky and the Chinese Dragon danced. All the children were delighted.

"The Fat Controller was right," tooted Percy. "Delivering coal is a very important job."

Did you enjoy the story?
Can you answer these questions?

1 What was Percy's job?

2 What were James and Emily pulling?

3 Who was Gordon pulling?

4 Who was stuck on the line because he didn't have any coal?